Miss Nussbaum

Mary Anne's Revenge

Other books by
Ann M. Martin

P.S. Longer Letter Later
(written with Paula Danziger)
Leo the Magnificat
Rachel Parker, Kindergarten Show-off
Eleven Kids, One Summer
Ma and Pa Dracula
Yours Turly, Shirley
Ten Kids, No Pets
Slam Book
Just a Summer Romance
Missing Since Monday
With You and Without You
Me and Katie (the Pest)
Stage Fright
Inside Out
Bummer Summer

THE KIDS IN MS. COLMAN'S CLASS series
BABY-SITTERS LITTLE SISTER series
THE BABY-SITTERS CLUB mysteries
THE BABY-SITTERS CLUB series
CALIFORNIA DIARIES series

Friends *Baby-sitters Club* Forever

(Mary Anne's Revenge)

Ann M. Martin

AN
APPLE
PAPERBACK

SCHOLASTIC INC.

New York Toronto London Auckland Sydney

Mexico City New Delhi Hong Kong

ISBN 0-590-52340-6

12 11 10 9 8 7 6 5 4 3 2 1   0 1 2 3 4 5/0

Printed in the U.S.A.   40

First Scholastic printing, March 2000

The author gratefully acknowledges
Nola Thacker
for her help in
preparing this manuscript.

Mary Anne's Revenge

❀ Chapter 1

I was surrounded by smoke. Thick, black, ashy coils of smoke curled up the walls and around my legs.

I ran to the door of my bedroom. But the door wasn't there. I turned and saw the fire reaching up the bureau, drawer by drawer. The curtains burst into flames. One by one, my favorite books exploded into a spookily merry blaze, like a scene from *Fahrenheit 451.*

I backed up, watching in disbelief.

Faintly, I could hear the wail of sirens.

My closet door swung open and my best dress began a fire dance of its own. I smelled leather cooking and knew my shoes were burning too.

I backed away and felt the doorknob against my back. It wasn't hot. The fire wasn't outside yet. All I had to do was turn the knob and step out to safety.

But I couldn't move. The flames seemed to laugh at me: snap, crackle, pop, *hahahahaha*.

A bottle of nail polish exploded on my dresser, and I jumped and choked out a scream as a little sheet of fire raced across the top of it.

"No!" I gasped as I saw the necklace Logan had given me glow molten red and then begin to melt. "No . . ."

Something brushed my leg and I screamed. The smoke felt like fur clinging to my legs.

I looked down. "Tigger!" I gasped. I had to save Tigger. I bent to scoop him up and staggered. A wave of dizziness washed over me.

For a horrifying second, as the floor rushed toward me, I thought I was falling. Then I realized that I wasn't falling — I was shrinking. In nanoseconds, I was eyeball-to-eyeball with my cat.

I stopped shrinking and put my hand against the door to steady myself. Down low, the smoke wasn't quite as thick and I could breathe a little easier.

The door.

I looked up. Way, way up. There was no way I could reach that doorknob.

There was no way I could get out. No way things could get worse.

But they could.

Because now Tigger was looking at me strangely. His eyes had narrowed. His tail was lashing. His ears were back. He crouched lower and I realized he was about to spring. At *me*.

I turned to run. I heard him leap and land with a thud behind me!

I spun around and shouted, "No, Tigger!" as I kicked out at him.

He dug his claws into my ankle. Hard.

"Me-OW!" He spat.

"OW!" I cried, and sat up in time to see the ghostly shape of my cat arc through the gray light of dawn as I kicked the covers and him up into the air. Landing with the softest of thumps, he disappeared under the desk.

"Tigger," I exclaimed. "I'm sorry! But I had such a bad dream!"

I looked around the still-unfamiliar room. Nothing was burning.

I sniffed cautiously. No smoke.

I looked down at myself. I wasn't a shrunken person.

My dream was just another version of the nightmares I'd had so often since the fire. I'd thought they were going away.

But clearly they weren't.

I pulled the covers around me, feeling cold and lonely and lost. "Tigger," I called softly.

But Tigger ignored me. I wondered if cats had nightmares. Did Tigger dream about the fire? Did he wonder what had happened in his old home and why he was living in a strange new house?

In spite of myself, my mind went back to the scene of the fire. I saw us standing in a little knot beneath the apple tree in the yard — Dad, Sharon, and me, clutching Tigger. I saw the fire trucks pulling to a stop, their lights piercing the night in an eerie reflection of the flames that swirled higher and higher through the house.

I smelled the smoke. I heard Sharon sobbing and my father murmuring softly to her. I felt his hand gripping my shoulder and realized that he'd saved my life. I looked down at Tigger, who, uncatlike, wasn't squirming in spite of the death grip I had on him. Maybe he realized that *I'd* saved *his* life.

I saw Mrs. Prezzioso in her purple bathrobe, trotting across the lawn toward us, her face alarmed and sympathetic.

And I almost did what I hadn't been able to do for the longest time after the fire. I almost started crying.

Stop it, I told myself.

Then I thought about Logan, my ex-boy[friend]. Had I done the right thing by breaking up with him? The answer was yes, but the question still wouldn't go away. Everything reminded me of Logan: videos, walks, books, the smell of french fries, the sports channel on television, my father's voice reading the baseball box scores aloud from the newspaper in the mornings to Sharon and me . . .

My cat.

When I broke up with Logan, I thought I'd get my life back. But it seemed as if my life had become just one more thing I'd lost. Everything that had helped define me was gone.

Life was not working out the way I had planned. I seemed to be rattling around in all the space I'd gotten when I'd split with Logan. I wasn't the all-new, totally confident, self-assured Mary Anne I had expected to be, the Mary Anne who wasn't described in terms of other people: Mary Anne Spier, daughter of Richard Spier, stepdaughter of Sharon Schafer Spier, stepsister of Jeff Schafer, and stepsister and best friend of Dawn Schafer, who lived in California. I was still all that, as well as the Mary Anne who was a resident of Stoneybrook, Connecticut, student at Stoneybrook Middle School, secretary of the Baby-sitters Club, ex-girlfriend of Logan, best friend of Kristy Thomas, good friend of Claudia Kishi and Stacey McGill and Abby Stevenson. But I still didn't know who I was.

It was as if I had become the tiny little person in my nightmare — the incredible shrinking Mary Anne.

❋ Chapter 2

"Not a wonderful Wednesday night?" Kristy asked sympathetically the next morning at school.

I raised heavy-lidded eyes and looked at her. "You can tell?" I asked.

"I can tell." Kristy charges through life like a soccer fullback and is not always the most perceptive person in the world. But she and I have been best friends since we were babies. We grew up next door to each other on Bradford Court before Kristy moved to her new stepfather's mansion and I moved with my dad and Sharon to our old (now burned down) farmhouse. So it wasn't surprising that she picked up on my flattened (or shrunken) frame of mind.

I closed my locker and sighed from the soles of my shoes. "I had a nightmare early this morning. I couldn't go back to sleep."

"Oh, no. I thought those weren't so bad any-more," Kristy said.

"They aren't." I managed a weak smile. "But when I do have them, they're pretty high on the special-effects scale."

"Oh, Mary Anne. Good grief." That was Kristy language for *That's terrible. Is there anything I can do?*

"It's like the fire has become quicksand," Kristy continued as we walked down the hall. "It's pulling you down. Keeping you from getting on with your life. You've got to fight back. Fight fire with fire, no pun intended."

"I guess," I said. I stopped outside the door of my next class. "I'll try."

"Good. See you at lunch." Kristy charged into the mob of students and disappeared down the hall.

At lunch, Kristy had all kinds of advice to offer me. Getting involved in sports was very high on her list of ways to get me out of my funk.

"Kristy," I said. "Have you ever seen me do any-thing more athletic than ride a bicycle?"

"Bicycling is good," Kristy plowed on. "You could train for a bike race. I could help. That would definitely refocus your energies."

"Thanks," I said, "but no thanks."

"But . . ."

"And sports remind me of Logan." This was true, because Logan was a sports maniac like Kristy. But it was more true that I didn't want Kristy deciding this was one of her brilliant ideas. Getting Kristy to let go of an idea is like getting a bone away from a dog.

"Oh. Well . . ." Fortunately the warning bell rang before Kristy could think of any more suggestions for returning me to "the confidence zone" (as she put it).

As I sat in the yearbook meeting after school that day, I was thinking about how Kristy somehow managed to stay in that zone. I've always loved yearbooks. They're history books and souvenirs and memory catchers, all rolled into one. I thought about how I loved looking at my dad's old high school yearbook and about how he and Sharon can be seen smiling out from some of the pages together, since that is when they first started dating.

Then I remembered that the old yearbooks — Dad's, Sharon's, and mine — were now just ashes. And then I told myself, *Stop it. You still have the memories. A fire can never burn those up.*

"Stop it!" Cokie Mason's sharp voice echoed my own thoughts, startling me into awareness. "Stop talking and pay *attention*!"

Cokie Mason is one of the people whose picture will be all over the yearbook — in no small part because she is one of the yearbook editors.

This, in my opinion, does not improve the yearbook one bit. When they were handing out kindness and decency, Cokie was probably in the bathroom fixing her makeup and telling her mirror image how much better she was than everybody else.

I know I sound mean, and I hate to be mean about anybody, but Cokie Mason is really one of the most totally un-nice people in the universe. She is petty and devious, and she tried to steal Logan from me more than once in a sneaky, underhanded way.

As one of two editors in chief of the yearbook, along with Rick Chow, Cokie has the right to tell everyone at the yearbook staff meeting to be quiet and listen. But it's hard for me to do so.

I wish Rick would take charge more, but Cokie has completely intimidated him. Mostly he nods and does what Cokie tells him to do (just like most of Cokie's friends, come to think of it).

I work on the features section of the yearbook with Abby Stevenson and Austin Bentley. Abby's a relative newcomer to the school and used to be a member of the Baby-sitters Club (or BSC). She stopped to concentrate on her athletic activities, primarily soccer. I was surprised when she joined the yearbook staff, but she told me she wanted to make sure that sports got a fair amount of coverage, "along with all those dances and things." Austin has been at SMS longer than Abby. He's named after two cars, and he laughs when people tease him about it. I know him a little because he's on the football team with Logan, and I like him because he hasn't acted weird around me — the way some people have — since Logan and I broke up.

"Okay," Cokie said, putting her hands on her hips. "That's better. This is what I think we should do: I think we should get ready to hold the vote for the Class Bests for the yearbook."

Rick nodded.

"Why?" asked Mariah Shillaber. She and Woody Jefferson are the yearbook copyeditors.

"Why?" Cokie repeated, looking surprised. "Because that's only the most important part of the yearbook. Voting for Funniest, Most Likely to Succeed, Best-Looking . . ."

"Nastiest," I heard Abby mutter under her breath. Then she raised her hand. "I don't think the results of a popularity contest should be the most important part of the yearbook."

Cokie frowned. She's not used to being challenged.

Before she could say anything, Woody said, "It doesn't have to turn into a mere popularity contest."

"How are you going to avoid it?" Abby asked.

"What's wrong with someone being chosen for something because she's popular?" Cokie demanded.

I didn't say anything. I didn't want to do this, in part because the Most and Best section is part of the features section, which means it would be up to Abby, Austin, and me to run the elections. That would be a huge amount of work. And it would take up chunks of the pages allotted to the section, pages that we'd already discussed using in what I thought were much more original ways.

Abby generally has a quick answer and she had one now. "Cokie," she said, "the yearbook is supposed to represent everybody, not just the kids who have the nicest teeth or best ears, like in some dog show."

"Dog show!" Cokie looked outraged.

Woody said, "It doesn't have to be a dog show, Abby. What we need to do to make it more student-friendly is add categories that will include all students, like Most Artistic, Most Creative, Most Likely to Accidentally Invent a Time Machine."

"Not a bad idea," Mariah said.

"And of course we'll keep Most Beautiful and the other important categories that everyone expects." Cokie sniffed.

Abby opened her mouth and Woody once again intervened. "I'm sure Cokie meant the other more *traditional* categories."

"Right," said Cokie. "Everyone in favor, hold up your hand."

I voted against it, and I wasn't the only one, but the overwhelming majority voted to have an expanded Most and Best section in the yearbook.

When the voting was over, Cokie looked at me and smiled her evil-politician smile. "It looks like you've got to do some *real* work in the features sections now, Mary Anne," she said.

"I just hate to see it take up space we could use for other features," I said, trying to sound neutral.

"Oh. I thought you were upset because you and Logan are no longer eligible for Best Couple," Cokie purred.

Several staffers laughed at that.

"Stuff it, Cokie," said Abby.

Cokie pretended she hadn't heard Abby.

I smiled weakly and tried to think of a comeback. But I couldn't. I felt about two inches tall.

The incredible shrinking Mary Anne was getting smaller by the minute.

❄ Chapter 3

"No, I'm upset because we'll have to use your picture in the Most Likely to Become an Ax Murderer category," I said. "No, but why don't you go jump in the lake? No, I'm not upset. . . . Yes, I am."

I was talking to myself. I admit it. I was setting the table and talking to myself.

I was trying to think of the perfect comeback for Cokie's spiteful remark. And so far I hadn't been able to do so, even though I'd been brooding all afternoon about what she'd said.

"Mary Anne?"

I looked up to see Sharon, my stepmother, standing in the doorway to the kitchen.

"Are you okay? Were you talking to yourself?"

"I guess I was," I said, feeling dumb.

Sharon smiled. "I hope it was a good conversation."

"So far, no."

"Well, we can make it three-way if you'll go get Richard. Dinner is ready."

I slid the last spoon into place and found my father in the tiny third bedroom of our rental house, which he was using as a study. He was sifting through a box of books.

He smiled warmly at me when I peered around the open door. "Hi," he said. "I'm telling you, I'll be glad when we're back in a house that has real bookshelves. Having to move these boxes around is driving me crazy."

My dad is a neatnik. In his old study, his books had been arranged by category and alphabetized. Now the books he'd gotten since the fire just sat in labeled boxes, except for a few of the main law books.

"Dinner's ready," I said.

"Good. I'm hungry." After he stood up and stretched, we walked back to the kitchen to help Sharon finish putting food out on the dining room table.

"Smells great," my dad said. "What is it?"

"Mixed-noodle casserole," Sharon replied. She looked pleased.

"What's that?" I asked. Sharon is kind of disorganized, which makes her an erratic cook. She's been known to put sugar into a dish instead of salt, season everything twice, or absentmindedly neglect to turn the oven off in time — or not turn it on at all.

The aroma rising from the casserole was good, though.

Sharon plopped a spoonful of mixed noodles onto my plate. I saw macaroni elbows, corkscrews, spirals, ziti, and ragged sheets of lasagna poking out of a tomato sauce spiked with broccoli, string beans, what might have been eggplant, and what looked like — lima beans?

"It's what was left in all those boxes of noodles mixed together with all the leftover vegetables we had. Plus a nice eggplant. And basil," Sharon explained.

"Sounds great," said my dad.

Cautiously, I took a bite. "Delicious," I said.

"Oh, I'm glad," said Sharon. "I was afraid I might have forgotten something."

"I like the nights you're the cook," my father said. "It's always an adventure."

Sharon laughed. She is so easygoing. She and my father are perfect for each other.

"I stopped by the house today," said Sharon.

"No kidding," my father teased gently. We're remodeling our old barn into a new house, and Sharon goes by there at least once a day to check on the progress.

"It looks fabulous," said Sharon. "The frame's finished now, and you can see where all the windows are going to be. Total light. It's going to be amazing."

"I can't wait," said my dad.

"I can't either," I heard myself say. "This house is too small."

"Too small?" said my father. "Well, I guess we could use more bookshelves."

Dad didn't understand. I meant that I was feeling crowded, even though I had a room of my own. My father had been acting like Super-Protective Dad since the fire. After we'd moved into our rental house, he seemed to check on me all the time, tapping on the door of my room to see how I was doing, asking me repeatedly where I was going and when I'd be back, even for something routine, such as a BSC meeting.

He wasn't as bad as he'd been when I was a little girl, but he was definitely getting on my nerves. And that made me feel bad, because I could understand why he was being so protective. After all, he'd lost everything but his family in the fire too.

Why did it have to be our house? My thoughts slipped back into the same old pattern. Why couldn't it have been the house of someone deeply mean and petty, like Cokie? Of course I didn't wish that Cokie's house had burned down, but maybe I did wish she'd had major smoke damage to all her clothes.

And then it came to me. The perfect comeback to Cokie's shot at the yearbook staff meeting that afternoon: "No, Cokie. I'm just upset because we'll have to have a page for you for Least Likely Ever to Be Part of a Couple."

I smiled, feeling better. I rehearsed it in my head, imagining her face if I'd actually had the nerve to say something that spiteful and mean. My smile widened.

"I thought you'd like my new surprise," my father said.

I returned to the conversation at the table. "Surprise?" I said.

"The new beds I bought. Yours has an antique pine headboard and footboard, carved with a leaf-and-vine-pattern trim. It'll be great in the new house."

"Oh," I said blankly.

"And we can get rid of this lumpy, plastic-wood rental bedroom furniture," said Sharon. "Super, Richard!"

My father beamed.

I said, "But Dad — I mean, the bed sounds great, but what if I wanted to pick out my own bed?"

My dad looked startled, a little less beamingly happy. "Of course. You can do that. We'll go by the store tomorrow and cancel the order and you can pick out whatever you want. There's no rush."

"No," I said. "Never mind."

"Really, Mary Anne . . ." he began.

"It's fine." I shrugged. "It's just a bed. Whatever."

We were all silent. I could tell I'd surprised both Sharon and my father. I wasn't a "whatever" kind of girl.

But maybe it was time I became one. Maybe it was time I stopped taking everything so seriously, worrying about everything being right. Maybe I should start taking things easy. Isn't that what Kristy had been trying to say to me?

Whatever.

�֍ Chapter 4

One thing about being the incredible shrinking Mary Anne — it's easy to be a spy. I spent all of the next day being an attitude-makeover spy at SMS.

That is, I kept quiet and observed my friends and fellow students at school. It was as if I were researching the kind of new attitude I wanted. Maybe you could even call it comparison shopping.

Since Cokie had already made an announcement about the vote over the loudspeaker during homeroom the next morning, I had even more of an opportunity for research. The moment after the loudspeaker squawked and died, everyone began to talk about who would or should win the votes. I heard Alan Gray discussed as a candidate for Funniest (I was sure Kristy would disagree). I heard Emily Bernstein, editor of the SMS school newspaper, spoken of as a sure thing for Most Intelligent. I also heard both Logan and Abby mentioned in the Most Athletic categories.

It was kind of funny, in a way, since the categories themselves hadn't been decided on yet. We were supposed to do that at a meeting of the yearbook staff that afternoon.

I heard the "who's who" buzz all day long. Even Kristy, Claudia, and Stacey were caught up in it. Stacey suggested that Claudia should be the only possible choice for Most Artistic. Claudia thought Stacey ought to be elected Most Intelligent *and* Most Beautiful. Kristy nominated herself (to me) as Most Likely to Be President of the World.

No one suggested I would be the most or best anything. I was just Mary Anne. I wasn't a sophisticated math whiz like Stacey. I wasn't artistic and free-spirited like Claudia. I wasn't athletic and outspoken like Abby. I wasn't presidential material, like Kristy. But maybe I could work on becoming more . . . well, something.

By the time I arrived at the yearbook meeting, I was so overwhelmed by how not Most and Best I was, and so amazed at how much thought and energy everybody was putting into the idea (especially the "traditional" categories) that I could only think about what an enormous job this was going to turn out to be. Then I heard Alan Gray talking about how lucky he was to be "naturally funny." He was campaigning! Grace Blume, Cokie's best friend and second-in-command, told everyone that in her opinion, people with "classic bone structure" such as Cokie would be the best choice to represent the class as Most Beautiful. It didn't take me long to figure out that Cokie herself was campaigning — through her loyal-but-not-too-bright friend.

And, of course, thinking about the work ahead, I saved a few other sour thoughts for Cokie, who had not only announced the election that morning but had told the school that the ballots would be handed out on Monday. That meant that Abby, Austin, and I would have to spend the weekend getting ballots, ballot boxes, and ballot collectors organized.

I came into the yearbook office to find that Cokie was still campaigning: ". . . a category like Most Likely to Become a Major Movie Star would make a nice new edition to the list," she was saying as I slid into a seat beside Abby. Then she tossed her head and added, "Being a photogenic and talented person helps, naturally."

Translation? *Choose me! Choose me! Choose me!*

Woody raised his hand and said evenly, "I think you're right, Cokie. I think we need to decide on the categories, both traditional and new. The sooner we do that, the sooner the features staff can get to work on the ballots."

Cokie looked smug and pleased, even though Woody hadn't actually agreed with what she was saying. In addition to being a very good-looking guy, Woody was a much smoother operator than I had realized.

The debate that followed was a long one. We agreed pretty quickly on the usual choices: Most Beautiful, Most Likely to Succeed, Most Intelligent, Best Athlete, Best Artist, Funniest, Best Couple, and so forth. Abby didn't succeed in convincing the staff that the title Most Beautiful should apply to both the boy and the girl chosen in that category. In the end we called it, as always, Most Beautiful and Most Handsome. Mariah, however, persuaded us to change Funniest to Wittiest. Since no one could ever mistake Alan Gray's gross-out antics for wit, I wondered if she had him in mind when she suggested the change.

The new categories caused a little more controversy. Cokie suggested several extremely mean ones, such as Most Likely to Go Directly to Jail Without Passing Go, and Most Likely to Be Chosen for a Complete Makeover.

But even Rick wouldn't go along with those.

Cokie looked irritated. "I was just trying to be funny," she said.

Cokie's idea of funny is, obviously, putting down someone else.

We did make a category for Most Likely to Be Elected President. Cokie and several of the others threw their votes to Most Fashionable, which we then changed to Class Style Setters.

Other categories included Most Likely to Travel to the Moon, Most Likely to be Seen in Dark Glasses in Beverly Hills, and Most Likely to Make a Million.

When we'd finally finished, Abby went to the computer and we got to work creating ballots.

"This isn't going to be so bad," Abby assured me.

"Yeah," I said. "But I still don't think people should campaign. It should be —"

I never got to finish what I was saying. Cokie had overheard me, and she went into attack mode.

"Oh, Mary Anne," she said loudly. "Did we forget to put in a category that you might win? Let's see.

What about Quietest Student . . . or Most Likely to *Completely* Disappear into the Background?"

As usual, Cokie's attempts at wit drew laughter.

Abby's hand froze on the mouse.

I felt my face flushing.

Cokie went on, "Or how about Least Likely to Keep a Good Boyfriend?"

"But Cokie," Abby shot back, "we already have Most Likely to Drive a Boyfriend Insane, for you."

The even-louder laughter that followed stopped Cokie long enough for me to take a deep breath, feel grateful for Abby's support, and try to think of a comeback myself. But before I could think of anything, Logan walked into the yearbook office.

Several other people laughed at this.

Abby bumped my elbow with her shoulder as if to say, *Don't worry. I've got it covered.*

Logan didn't even look in my direction. That hurt. We hadn't spoken much since the breakup, and I'm not sure what I expected. I couldn't help remembering, though, how not so long ago, I was the first person Logan looked for whenever he walked into a room.

Now he made me feel invisible. Again.

"Hi, Rick," Logan said. "I brought these photos by for the yearbook."

"Thanks," Rick said, taking an envelope from him and opening it.

"There are two editors of the yearbook, you know," Cokie said, putting her hand on Logan's arm. Logan glanced at her, then at her hand. "Hi, Cokie," he said. "I know."

"These look good," Rick said.

I wanted to see the photos, but I remained rooted to the spot.

"Good? They're excellent," Cokie gushed. She used her other hand to run one pink-polished finger-nail down the edge of the photograph. "You've got such an eye, Logan."

"You think so? Thanks."

"We'll have to find some more work for you. The yearbook needs your kind of creativity." Cokie smiled at Logan. "I'm about to leave. Maybe you could walk me to my locker and we could talk about it."

"No problem," said Logan. "I have to go to my locker too."

Cokie shot me a triumphant glance from under her lowered eyelashes. Then she and Logan left.

He still hadn't looked in my direction.

"I'd like to use her head for a soccer ball and practice penalty shots against a wall," said Abby.

"Logan didn't seem to mind," I replied miserably.

"I didn't see any enthusiasm on his part. But even Logan isn't immune to disgusting flattery."

Austin cleared his throat. "Is this a private conversation? Should I go away?" he asked.

"No," I said. "Let's get to work. I'd like to get the ballots over with."

I didn't add that, more than anything, I wanted to crawl home. Cokie had made her point. It was Cokie's world, and I was just living in it.

✽ Chapter 5

I didn't get to stay home Friday night and brood over my lack of Most and Best qualities, Cokie's lack of human qualities, or anything else. I'd forgotten that I had promised Kristy we'd spend Friday night at the movies.

I tried to get out of it. Then I tried to persuade Kristy that we should rent videos and stay in — at her house, since it's larger than our rental.

"Are you kidding?" Kristy said. "Even if I could get to the VCR, which I can't, this place is a zoo. Karen is having a sleepover, remember?"

I'd forgotten. (Karen is Kristy's seven-year-old stepsister.)

"Anyway, I've got extra bucks burning a hole in my pocket. I want to waste it on overpriced tickets for the ghost movie they made from that old TV series and even more on overpriced popcorn, extra butter."

"Ugh," I said.

"So I won't share. Just don't beg me later. I'll see you at six forty-five, fifteen minutes before showtime, out in front of the theater. Be there."

She hung up.

I hung up.

Kristy was soooo bossy. Why couldn't I tell her to leave me alone?

"So Abby tells me you had a nasty encounter of the Cokie kind," Kristy said later, as I sulked up to the movie theater entrance.

"Leave me alone," I snapped.

"Ah. A *really* nasty encounter."

I didn't answer. We bought our tickets. Kristy bought her popcorn. We went into the theater.

Kristy headed for the left center of a row in the back.

I stopped in the aisle.

"What?" asked Kristy.

"You might ask where *I* want to sit," I said. "What am I, invisible?"

Looking bewildered, Kristy said, "We always sit in the same place. But if you want to sit somewhere else . . ."

"No. The same old place is fine." I followed her in and plopped down in the seat. "I don't understand why they have to remake perfectly good old movies. But it's even dumber to remake crummy old TV shows."

"Hey, this used to be a pretty good television show."

"So why ruin it with a terrible movie?"

"I liked the *Brady Bunch* movies," Kristy went on.

I couldn't help but smile. " 'Marcia, Marcia, Marcia,' " I replied, quoting a line from the movie.

"Exactly."

My smile disappeared. "How about 'Cokie, Cokie, Cokie'? You should have seen her, Kristy. She attached herself to Logan like, well, like the slime she is. She is disgusting. And she practically called me a mousy little freak. And I couldn't think of one thing to say."

"Cokie has that effect on lots of people," Kristy assured me.

"She makes me so angry." I was fuming, my voice getting louder. "I'd like to push her into a locker and leave her there."

"Oooh, nasty."

"A gym locker," I elaborated. "Filled with old, disgusting, sweaty gym clothes."

"Now you're talking," Kristy said. "You know, Mary Anne, it's nice to see your dark side coming out."

I stopped. "Am I being too mean?"

"Are you kidding? How could anybody be too mean about Cokie? Especially after what she said to you. You have every right to be totally infuriated with her."

"Good."

The houselights went down.

I folded my arms. "And now we have to sit through *hours* of dumb advertisements and movie trailers," I said.

"You go, Mary Anne," cheered Kristy. She thrust the popcorn toward me. "Here, you can even have some popcorn to keep up your strength."

"Thanks," I said. "I think I will."

The next morning I woke up feeling grouchy and mean. Was this how Cokie felt all the time? In a way, I enjoyed it. It was such an unusual feeling. Breakfast cheered me up a little. Since it was Saturday, I could stay home and be me.

Whoever me was.

Unfortunately, my father had different ideas.

"I was thinking about what you said about picking out your own furniture, Mary Anne, and I've decided you're right."

The old Mary Anne would have said, "That's great, Dad."

The new, mean Mary Anne said (to herself), "Duh."

"So Sharon and I have decided that what we need is a house tour."

"We're going to tour our new house? Again?" I said.

"No. We're going on a real house tour. The Greenvale Historic House Tour. It'll give us some great ideas."

There went my quiet Saturday at home.

I looked around the kitchen, wincing at the ugly wallpaper. Maybe I *didn't* want to spend the day in this house.

"Okay," I said. I know I sounded less than enthusiastic, and I saw Dad's eyebrows pull together in a quick frown. But Sharon rushed in to say, "Terrific! There's a great new restaurant there, I hear, and if we have time we can check out some of the antique shops."

"Shopping? Oh, no!" My father groaned, pretending to be dismayed.

"I'll go get ready," I said, standing up.

Sharon was prepared for the trip. When I got into the car I discovered she'd brought a camera, a notebook, a pen and a pencil, and a plastic zipper file to put catalogs, folders, and business cards in.

"What's all that for?" I asked.

"Research," explained Sharon. "I can take notes, photograph furniture I like, and save everything for reference."

"I'm impressed," my father said. "And maybe a little afraid."

Greenvale is about thirty miles from Stoneybrook. It's a classic New England town, with old houses, big trees, stone walls lining every narrow, winding road — and lots of tourists with cameras slung around their necks.

My dad finally found a parking space, bought tickets for the tour of the nine houses, and led us into the tourist herd.

It was sort of fun, at first. But how many old houses can you walk through?

Lots, apparently, if you are Sharon and my father. By the fifth house, I was tired. Sharon was still going strong and my father was perfectly happy to follow the rest of the crowd from room to room, admiring this Queen Anne table and that well-preserved rug.

I lagged farther and farther behind until, after the sixth house, I said, "I can't go on."

"What? Are you all right?" My father swung around and put his hand on my forehead as if I were a little kid.

I jerked away. "I'm fine," I said, speaking more loudly than I had intended. "I'm just tired of walking through old houses."

"Only three more," Sharon said.

"Why don't I just wait here?" I suggested. I gestured toward a wooden bench under a sprawling oak tree.

"No," my father said. "We can't leave you all alone out here."

"I won't be alone. There are millions of people around." There were a lot of people, all waiting patiently in line for their turn to *ooh* and *ahh* their way through the house.

"We're in a strange town," my father said. "I don't want to abandon you."

"You won't be abandoning me. I'll stay right here. I promise. And my feet really hurt."

"She'll be fine, Richard," Sharon said.

My father didn't listen. "I'm not going to leave you alone," he said.

"No one's going to kidnap me! And I'm not going to go off with some stranger offering me candy. I'll be fine. I'm thirteen years old!"

But my father was shaking his head. "I'll stay with you."

"Richard —" Sharon protested.

I didn't give her a chance to finish. "NO!" I said, so loudly that heads turned. "Leave me alone. I'm not a baby. Okay?"

My father's face became perfectly blank. He looked at me as if I were a stranger.

I don't think I had shouted at him like that since I was much, *much* younger. And that had been little-kid shouting, not like this.

After a long, long moment, he said, "Fine. Stay right here on that bench. Don't move."

He was still treating me like a little kid. Horrified that I had shouted at my dad, and angry that he wouldn't listen, I walked stiffly to the bench and sat down.

Dad and Sharon approached the house. Although I wasn't sure, I thought Sharon gave me a sympathetic glance as they walked through the door.

At each of the last two houses, I waited outside. My feet weren't hurting as badly anymore, but I didn't want to spend any more time with my father.

Sharon kept up a bright conversation on the trip back to Stoneybrook. Dad and I tried to avoid speaking to each other, even when we stopped to pick up a pizza for an early dinner.

When we got home, I ate one piece of pizza, then went to my room and stayed there.

Late that night as I drifted uneasily toward sleep, dreading another nightmare and feeling awful about the day, I heard the murmur of my dad and Sharon talking in their bedroom.

I turned over, turned again, sat up, thumped my pillow, and stopped as I caught the sound of my name: ". . . mumble, mumble, Mary Anne . . ."

I put my ear to the wall. My father's voice went on. "I don't know what's come over her, Sharon. She's so moody. Everything I say is wrong. I can't do anything right."

"She's a thirteen-year-old girl, Richard. Moodiness is expected. You should have seen me when I was thirteen."

Good old Sharon, I thought.

My father said, "It's like I hardly know her. I

can't believe she's my own little Mary Anne sometimes."

Little. I'm not little, I thought. I thumped my pillow and lay down again, angry once more. I wasn't
anybody's little girl.

The new Mary Anne had finally arrived.

✳ Chapter 6

I had planned to walk to school with Claudia on Monday morning. As I was leaving, my father said, "You're walking to school by yourself?"

"With Claudia," I said. "I'm meeting her outside her house."

"Oh."

I had a feeling that he was peering out the window at me until Claudia came running down her front steps to join me.

I didn't look back, though.

Claudia looked as fabulous as ever. She was wearing wide-legged purple pants cut off at the ankle, flat black shoes, striped socks (purple and white), and a white cropped top over a purple camisole. She'd pulled her hair back with papier-mâché decorated combs that she'd created herself: two little figures were holding onto the combs as if they were being blown backward. It was pretty funny. And very creative.

I felt kind of dull in my jeans and sweater. But I had to admit that even if I wanted to, I couldn't pull off Claudia's look. It was unique.

"Definitely Best Artist," I said, surveying her outfit.

"You think?" she said, slinging her (hand-painted) canvas bag over her shoulder. "It'd be nice. Probably impress my parents. Not as much as good grades, of course, but . . ."

Claudia was trying to be cool and uninterested about the possibility of being elected Best Artist, but I could tell she was thrilled by the idea.

I wondered how it would feel to be considered an automatic candidate for best anything.

As we walked up the front steps to SMS, heads turned in our direction.

"You see," I said. "People are saying 'There's Claudia Kishi, Best Artist.'"

Claudia laughed. More heads turned.

Several pairs of heads drew closer together and I could tell people were talking about us.

Claudia stopped smiling. She looked puzzled. "Somehow," she said, "I think they're talking about us. But not in a good way, if you know what I mean."

"I think I do," I said as several more heads turned our way and someone giggled and then stopped abruptly, as if she'd had to clap her hand over her mouth.

We walked in the front door and almost collided with Stacey.

"Whoa," Claudia said. She shook her head. "Running in the hall is a very serious infraction of the rules, young lady. . . ."

Stacey ignored her. "Never mind that. Have you heard what they're saying? No, I can tell you haven't."

"What?" asked Claudia.

Stacey looked at me. "Over here," she said, and pulled us into a corner that was out of sight of most of the students coming in.

"I heard it from Pete Black," Stacey said. "He heard it from Austin, who heard it from Grace Blume."

"What? *What?*" Claudia practically screamed.

"They're saying that Mary Anne begged Logan to take her back and he said no. He told her he was in love with someone else. He wouldn't tell her who it was . . ."

"No way!" Claudia's voice rose in outrage.

My mouth had dropped open. I couldn't seem to force any words out.

Stacey went on. "And when you heard that, Mary Anne, you became totally deranged and wrote Logan dozens of e-mails and left him a gazillion desperate messages. . . . In fact, it was so bad that his parents are thinking of getting a new, unlisted number."

I found my voice. But all I could manage to say was, "Who would make up such a stupid story?"

"Well, considering that Grace is Cokie's puppet, I think the culprit is pretty clear," Claudia said.

"It's not true. Not one single word of it," I said.

"Of course not," said Stacey. "But the question is, what are you going to do about it?"

The warning bell rang.

We stepped out into the hall. I stayed between Claudia and Stacey, feeling very exposed.

And then I saw Logan.

I stopped. He stopped. My face turned seven shades of embarrassment-red.

Logan had clearly heard the story too. He ducked his head, turned, and walked rapidly away from us.

I sagged against Claudia's shoulder. I felt beaten.

I wanted to cry. Tears stung my eyes.

But I kept them back by thinking about how good Cokie would feel if I started crying in front of everybody.

Kristy barreled up to us. Her face was livid. "She's a vicious pig, Mary Anne. And that's the nicest thing I can say about her."

I kept my lips pressed together and blinked back the tears.

Not noticing, Kristy continued. "Revenge. Revenge is the only solution. You've been nice too long. We've all been. Being nice to subhuman specimens like Cokie just allows them to be meaner. Someone's got to stop her."

"Sounds good," I managed to say.

Kristy pounded her fist into her hand. "She's going to be sorry she was ever born."

"Sounds even better," Stacey put in.

The second bell rang. We headed for homeroom.

I was so upset, I'd forgotten about the Most and Best election until our teacher started handing out the ballots. I looked down at mine and hoped that Cokie wouldn't be elected anything. Then I picked up my pen and voted for Claudia as Best Artist, Stacey as Class Style Setter (female), Abby for Best Athlete (female), Logan for Best Athlete (male), Cary

Retlin as Most Likely to Travel to the Moon, and Kristy as Most Likely to Be Elected President.

The teacher took our ballots and handed them over to Cokie, who was collecting them with Rick Chow. It was a typical Cokie division of labor. She got to swoop around the halls, smiling and waving and collecting the ballots, while the features staff — namely me, Austin, and Abby — got to stay after school to count them.

Cokie's eyes met mine as she took the ballot box from our teacher. She smiled a big, evil grin.

I remained calm, even though Cokie's expression had just told me everything I needed to know.

Cokie had definitely been the one to start the rumor.

I spent my next class making a list of revenge possibilities. Trying to get Cokie kicked out of school seemed a little extreme, so I left that off. But I did come up with:

Put glue in her locker lock.
Glue her books to her locker floor.
Put glue in her gym shoes.
Put a dead rat in her pack.
Put two dead rats in her pack.
Give her a piece of laxative gum.

Of course, I didn't know where I would find one dead rat, let alone two, and I knew I'd never touch one if I did. I wasn't sure how I could get into Cokie's locker. And if Cokie had any sense, she'd never accept a piece of gum from me.

But glue in her gym shoes had some potential, I thought.

At lunch Kristy flourished a piece of paper at us and said, "Guess what this is."

Claudia tilted her head, trying to read the page. "Answers to a test?"

"No. A list of ways to get revenge on Cokie."

"You're kidding. Kristy, I made a list too!" I pulled out my notebook, flipped it open, and showed her the page.

"Excellent. Let's see what we've got."

Kristy's read:

Call Cokie, convince her she won the lottery, then tell her the truth after she's made an even bigger fool of herself.

Drop a snail in her water at lunch when she's not looking.

Write fake letters to the Love Advice column in the Stoneybrook newspaper and sign her name.

Write fake letters from Logan to her.

Hide her homework.

"Well, you both have good stuff here," said Stacey. "But I think some of it is too complicated."

"And some of it is too childish," I said.

"You're right," said Kristy. "But this was a spur-of-the-moment list. With thought and planning, I'm sure we can have Cokie regretting all her evil ways."

"I hope so," I said.

"We'll pursue this further," Kristy promised. She raised a forkful of salad and inspected it. "Hmmm. Unappetizing, brown at the edges, and soaked in a salad dressing that looks like an oil slick . . . I'm sure we'll find inspiration *everywhere* for getting back at Cokie."

I lifted a forkful of salad. "Revenge," I said solemnly.

"Revenge," Kristy, Claudia, and Stacey repeated.

Now all we needed was a foolproof plan.

❋ Chapter 7

Feeling slightly better, maybe even cheered a little by thoughts of revenge (put gum in her hair — no, put *glue* in her hair) as I walked toward the yearbook office after school, I practically ran into Logan before I saw him.

I stopped. Thoughts of revenge fled. All thoughts fled. I blushed and began to turn away.

"Mary Anne," Logan said. "Wait."

Slowly, I turned around to face him. "What?"

"I'm on my way to baseball practice."

"I know." I would have known even if he hadn't had his gear with him. I knew Logan's schedule.

"Yeah, I guess you do." He managed a sort of twisted smile. "Listen, could we talk for a minute?"

"Now? I'm on my way to —"

"The yearbook office. I know." He paused. "This won't take long."

I leaned against a locker. "Okay," I said.

Logan didn't put a hand on the locker next to my shoulder as he'd done when we were going out. He fiddled with his glove.

"I heard the rumors that are going around," he began.

"Me too," I said.

"I'm sorry."

"It's not your fault."

"I know that. But I want you to know that I'm telling everybody what a pack of lies it is. And I wanted to make sure you're okay."

My throat tightened. Logan, even though he wasn't *my* Logan anymore, was just as kind and sweet as ever.

"I'm fine, thanks. Kristy and everyone have been there for me." The thought of the lists Kristy and I made eased the tightness in my throat somewhat.

"I thought they might have. Good."

I straightened up. "You're okay too?"

Logan nodded.

"Well, thanks for asking," I said, preparing to leave.

"Wait," he said. "There's one more thing. That huge lie had one sort of true thing in it. . . ."

I knew what he was going to say before he even said it.

"There is someone else. . . ."

My heart almost stopped. *Not Cokie*, I prayed.

"It's Dorianne Wallingford. . . . Mary Anne, are you sure you're okay?" A worried crease appeared between Logan's eyebrows.

I realized I'd sagged against the lockers — in relief at hearing Dorianne's name. I straightened again. "Dorianne's nice," I managed to say.

"I'm not sure if it's friendship or what," Logan said. "It's too soon, I guess. But we've been hanging out lately and I just wanted to let you know."

I felt my heart squeeze. Logan was interested in someone else. Of course, he was free to do whatever he wanted. But it made me feel sad. Somehow I managed to say, "Logan, I'll always care about you, and I think this is a good thing. I hope it works out."

"Yeah?" Logan peered at me. "Really?"

"Really," my voice said without a quiver. My lips smiled. "Thanks for telling me. And I'm glad we talked."

"Me too," said Logan.

"Well, I've got to go. We have to count those ballots, you know." My voice sounded a little too peppy to me, but Logan didn't seem to notice.

"See you around," he said.

"See you," I murmured.

I walked toward the office. I listened to his footsteps retreat down the hall. Just before I turned the corner, I looked over my shoulder and watched until Logan was out of sight.

That's that, I thought, and zombie-walked the rest of the way to the yearbook office. I took a deep breath, put on a neutral expression, and entered the room.

Austin and Abby were sitting at the table, boxes stacked in front of them. "There you are," said Austin. "Come on, start counting."

I dropped my pack on the floor and sat down. I pulled a ballot box toward me — and realized that Cokie was in the room too. She came out from one of the computer stations and said, "You're late, Mary Anne."

I felt Abby's scrutiny. My neutral expression hadn't been as neutral as I'd thought. Clearly some misery was showing on my face.

Cokie saw it too. I swear I saw her eyes light up. "Are you all right, Mary Anne?" she asked with fake concern.

"I'm fine, thank you." My hands fluttered uselessly among the slips of paper.

"You certainly don't look it," Cokie purred. "You look *awful*."

Suddenly, I couldn't take it anymore. I felt my eyes blaze with rage. I stood up and faced Cokie. "Well, it takes one to know one, doesn't it, Cokie? And you of all people ought to know about awful, because in my opinion, when they were handing out awful, you were first in line."

Cokie actually took a step back.

Austin scooted his chair a little away from the table, as if he were afraid we were going to start throwing things.

Abby said, "Mary Anne?"

Without another word, Cokie whirled around and stomped out of the office.

Austin said, "Wow, Mary Anne. You don't hear someone talking like that to Cokie every day."

"No," I said. I was shaking. I'd stood up for myself. Literally. I sat down again.

"Impressive," said Abby. "I'd say you just won a major battle. Wait till I tell everyone that Mary Anne Spier silenced Cokie Mason!"

"Thank you," I said.

I'd won the battle. But I wasn't sure about the war. Cokie would strike back. I was sure of that.

But this time I'd be prepared.

✳ Chapter 8

As we counted the Most and Best votes, my hands gradually stopped shaking. I found it soothing to sort the votes into boxes. As soon as we finished sorting all the votes by category, we would begin to count them.

The yearbook office seemed a little busier than usual. Staffers drifted in and out. I got some interested glances, and my cheeks burned as I remembered the spiteful rumor Cokie had spread about me. But it soon became apparent that people were, for the moment, more interested in how the vote count was going.

As we'd agreed before we started counting, we just smiled and shook our heads when people asked us who was winning.

"Not yet," Austin would say.

"It's not fair to say anything until we're finished," Abby would add.

I'd nod, keeping my head down. Cokie didn't reappear, but I was aware of Grace in hover mode until Abby said, sharply, "Are you trying to look over my shoulder, Grace? Because in a classroom, that would be called cheating."

"I'm not doing anything wrong," Grace whined, but she moved away to sit down at one of the computer terminals.

When we were about halfway through the count, a terrible truth began to dawn on me. Cokie's campaign to be elected everything seemed to be working. Not only that, but her less-than-lovely crowd of friends was racking up the votes too. When we'd finished, Katie Shea, a Cokie puppet who has less talent in her whole body than Claudia has in her little finger, beat Claudia for Best Artist. Cokie, whose fashion sense consists of spending as much money as possible on clothes, edged Stacey out for Class Style Setter. Not only that, she was voted Most Likely to Succeed — over Emily Bernstein — by four votes.

And she swept the Biggest Flirt Category.

We finished the count in stunned silence.

Abby looked across at me. "How can this be?" she demanded.

"We need to recount, of course," said Austin. "We should all take different categories."

Grace chose that moment to pop up. "Who won?" she asked.

"Nobody yet," Abby said grimly. "Go away."

Grace opened her mouth. Abby shot her a Look. Grace got the message and went back to the computer.

We counted again. Twice. We got the same results each time.

Then I realized something.

"Hey," I said, "you know what? My ballot isn't in here."

"How do you know?" Austin asked.

"Well, I didn't see anything with my handwriting or with my votes. But more than that, I used my green pen, and not a single ballot I've seen is written in green."

"Interesting," said Austin.

Even as he spoke, Abby had started to go through the ballots. "Mine's not here either," she said after a few minutes.

"How do you know?" asked Austin.

"Easy," Abby said with a cocky grin. "I voted for myself six times."

If it hadn't been so serious, I would have laughed out loud. I wondered what Abby had voted herself for.

But this was no laughing matter. "I haven't seen anything with Kristy's handwriting," I said. "I'd know her handwriting anywhere. Or Claudia's. And I know she used her purple pen and her red pen because those were her lucky colors for the day."

"Nothing like that in here," Austin said after looking through the piles.

"Plus, she would have misspelled at least one name," Abby added with an affectionate smile. (Claudia is a notoriously bad speller.)

"I think this is my ballot," Austin said.

"Yeah, but we have at least four unaccounted for," I pointed out.

"*And* a suspicious number of votes . . ." Abby began.

"I'm sure there's a reasonable explanation," Austin said, interrupting her although he didn't sound all that convinced.

The door of the office slid shut and I looked up to see Grace slipping out of the room. She hadn't asked who won this time. *Interesting,* I thought.

Whenever we have a vote, the teachers count the ballots in their homerooms, then write the number on the ballot boxes with their initials.

When we added up the numbers on the sides of the ballot boxes and then the number of actual votes counted, we were twenty votes short.

"Ballots are missing," said Abby firmly. "I think it's pretty clear what happened here."

"A fix," said Austin. "Great. Now we have to tell Mr. Fiske."

Mr. Fiske is our yearbook adviser. He hadn't been in school that day — which may have been why Cokie thought she could get away with fixing the election.

"First thing tomorrow morning," Abby said. "I can be here early."

"Me too," I chimed in.

"I can't," said Austin, looking just a little relieved. "Dentist appointment."

Going to the dentist almost sounded better than having to tell Mr. Fiske our suspicions. He was going to be upset by this.

But it had to be done. We couldn't let Cokie get away with it.

"What about the ballots?" asked Abby. "They're evidence. We don't want to leave them around."

"We can lock them in our lockers," I said. "We'll split them between the two of us, Abby. That way all the boxes will fit."

Abby nodded. "Let's do it."

Mr. Fiske wasn't in his room when we got there the next morning, which meant he was probably in the yearbook office. Abby and I got the ballot boxes from our lockers and headed for the office.

We found him. We also found Cokie.

"There you are," she said. "So who won?"

How could she act as if everything were normal?

Abby and I ignored Cokie. I looked at Mr. Fiske and we set the boxes on his desk. "We have a problem," I said.

"What?" asked Cokie. She was convincing. So convincing that I might have given her the Best Sleazy Actor award.

Still pretending that Cokie wasn't in the room, Abby said bluntly, "It looks like this election has been fixed."

"No way!" Cokie exclaimed. "What did you do?"

Looking upset, Mr. Fiske raised one hand as if to stop us from telling him. Then he dropped it. "Tell me what happened."

"When Cokie gave us the ballots yesterday,

Abby, Austin, and I counted them. Three times. Abby and I realized that our own ballots weren't in there. When we compared the number of ballots recorded as being collected by the teachers to the number of ballots we counted, we discovered that we were twenty ballots short."

"I never touched those ballots!" Cokie said. "Ask Rick! You're just slandering me, Mary Anne, because you're jealous."

"Get real," said Abby witheringly. "Who would be jealous of you?"

Before Cokie could answer, Mr. Fiske said, "These accusations will not help. We have no way of actually proving anything about anybody." He paused. He studied Cokie for a long moment.

She tried hard to look innocent. This time she wouldn't have won any awards.

"We should have a revote," I said.

"No!" cried Cokie. "That's not fair!"

"Why not?" asked Abby. "You don't even know who won . . . unless you know something about those votes that only Austin, Mary Anne, and I should know."

That stopped Cokie. But if looks could kill, Abby would have dropped dead at that instant.

Mr. Fiske said, "Under my direct supervision, we'll reprint the ballots. I will also supervise this time." He paused and consulted his calendar and then went on. "We'll have the revote next Monday morning. After the voting, I'll collect the boxes and keep them locked up until it's time to count the ballots."

"This is ridiculous," huffed Cokie.

"I see no alternative," said Mr. Fiske. By the way he said it, even Cokie could tell that the decision was final.

As we left the office, Cokie said to me, just softly enough so Mr. Fiske couldn't hear, "Loser."

Once that would have hurt my feelings. But not this time. I smiled at her. "We'll see who the loser is," I answered. I left the room before she could reply.

When the announcement came over the loudspeaker that morning saying that another vote for Most and Best would be held, heads turned in my direction. The kids in my homeroom knew I had been involved in the election.

The old Mary Anne wouldn't have wanted to talk about what happened. The new Mary Anne —

well, she didn't want to talk about it either. But if I didn't, Cokie would get away with her dishonest behavior.

So when Howie Johnson said, "Ooh, Mary Anne. Weren't you able to count high enough to include all the ballots?" I didn't turn away and roll my eyes like I once would have.

And when Emily Bernstein stopped by my locker and said, "What gives with the new election? Is it something I can use in the school newspaper?" I didn't say, "No comment."

I laid out the evidence. I knew Howie, with his big mouth, would spread it around immediately.

And even when Emily shook her head regretfully and said, "I'm not sure it's something I can *print*, but thanks for the information," I felt sure that Emily and her friends wouldn't just let Cokie take the election and run with it.

I was even more sure when Emily told me that afternoon that Cokie was spreading the rumor that I was trying to steal the election. "She tried to pretend it was because Logan likes her and not you, but *I* know better than that."

Emily's sharp. She watched me to see what my reaction would be. I nodded. "It's true. Logan and I are friends now and we talked about it. And, of course, Logan feels sorry for Cokie, trying so hard to get his attention when it's useless."

Emily's lip curled. "Gotcha," she said, and pushed off to her next class.

When Kristy, Claudia, Stacey, and I got together for our Monday afternoon BSC meeting, we discovered that we had been engaged in a sort of Stop Cokie! campaign. That is, we'd all been telling the truth about how Cokie had tampered with the voting in order to make sure she and her friends had won.

"You know," said Kristy, "I've had no trouble at all convincing people Cokie is up to no good. The moment they realize it's Mary Anne's word against Cokie's, they side with you, Mary Anne. Abby told me the same thing."

"Most trustworthy," agreed Claudia. "That's you, Mary Anne. Among other things."

"Most likely to give Cokie what she deserves, these days," said Kristy.

I blushed but I accepted it as a compliment. It felt good to be fighting back. "Thanks," I said. "But you know, I wouldn't mind making my revenge a little more complete. I mean, something more along the lines of all the awful things you and I put on our lists, Kristy."

Kristy got a thoughtful look on her face. "You mean that?" she asked.

"I do."

"Then there is only one thing to do. Talk to the master of practical jokes and diabolical schemes," Kristy pronounced.

"Who?" I asked.

"Cary Retlin, of course."

❄ Chapter 9

Cary Retlin is a mystery student, a cute guy who believes, in his own words, that "complications make life more interesting." He also believes in making the complications himself and is, according to Kristy, one of the sneakiest, cleverest people around.

I don't know about that, but I do know that Cary seems to have no limit to his skills. He can open lockers, has slipped the watch off Kristy's arm without her being aware of it, and is probably behind more of the jokes and puzzles that occur around SMS than anyone realizes.

Since Cary has also included the BSC in more than one of his pranks, I was a little worried when I finally tracked him down between classes on Tuesday morning. What if he thought Cokie's schemes and lies were just more of those complications that add interest to life?   .

"Cary?" I said. He closed his locker and turned his brown eyes in my direction.

"Hey, Mary Anne," he said. He shifted his books and I involuntarily tightened my grip on mine, as if he might magically make them disappear from my arms. "What's happening?"

"A lot. And I need your help."

"Oh?"

"Oh, yes." I told him everything that had been happening. I had a feeling he was more than up to speed on recent events, but he listened without interrupting.

"And so what I want is to teach Cokie a lesson," I concluded. "To stop her from getting away with fixing the election. To get *revenge*."

"Cokie," said Cary. "Now, *there* is one of life's complications."

My heart sank. Was Cary going to side with Cokie? "Kristy said you were the one to talk to," I added.

"Did she?" The corners of Cary's eyes crinkled, and he looked both pleased and amused. "Well, Kristy's never wrong, is she?"

"Does that mean you'll help?"

"Life's complications should be interesting," Cary pronounced. "Not . . ." He paused, seeming to search for a word. "Not sordid, petty, and unimaginative. I'm afraid Cokie is all three. Yes, I'll help. Any ideas?"

I slipped from my pack the two lists that Kristy and I had made and handed them to Cary. He glanced over them in a very professional manner, like a teacher eyeballing a test. "Hmmm," he said.

I waited.

Cary said, "Are you free after school?"

I nodded.

"Good. Meet me at the SMS library then." Cary folded the lists and stuck them into a pocket.

"We're going to research revenge?" I asked.

"You'll see," said Cary, ever the mystery man, and he walked away.

Cary was waiting when I arrived at the library that afternoon. He was reading magazines. From the stack next to him, I could tell he'd been reading for awhile.

"Am I late?" I asked, even though I knew I wasn't.

"No. Grab a stack of magazines from the rack and bring them to the table so we can get started."

Puzzled, I dumped my backpack on a chair and did what Cary had said. He thumbed the pages of his magazine and pulled out three subscription cards. He also found a page of three more that he tore out.

"Six," he said. "Not bad."

It was then that I realized he was reading *Seventeen*. This is not what you would expect a guy to be reading. But then, Cary isn't a typical guy.

"How many are in that magazine you're holding?" Cary asked.

I looked down. *Popular Mechanics*.

I found four subscription cards. I caught on. Sort of. "You want all the subscription cards from all these magazines?"

"Right."

I decided not to give Cary the satisfaction of begging him for answers. "Okay," I said, and went to work.

In a very short time we had about a hundred subscription cards. After we'd put the magazines back, Cary divided the cards in half and pushed one stack toward me.

"Now we fill in Cokie's name and address on every one of these cards."

"I don't have Cokie's address," I began, but Cary was ahead of me. He slapped a 3x5 card down in front of me and I saw that all the information I needed was neatly printed on it.

"Let's get to work," he said.

"We're ordering subscriptions to all these magazines for . . ." I looked around and lowered my voice even though no one was near, ". . . *her?*"

"That's the idea."

I liked it. I liked it a lot. I got to work, being careful to disguise my handwriting.

When we'd finished, I said, "There's a mailbox at the corner. Or I can go to the post office. It's not closed yet. . . ."

"Stop." Cary shuffled the thick stack of subscription cards into a neat pile, then wound a rubber band around them. He handed me the cards. "You don't mail them. You hold on to them."

"But . . ."

"The First Law of Revenge. Always have a secret weapon to fall back on. You can mail these anytime, and there is nothing Cokie can do to stop you."

"But until I mail them, she won't even know that I'm fighting back," I protested.

"This is for confidence," Cary told me. "You can jam her up with her own medicine later. I promise."

I would have continued arguing, but it was getting late. Slowly I nodded, then tucked the cards into the outside pocket of my pack, where they bulged out like a wad of chewing gum in a little kid's cheek. It was sort of comforting to know they were there.

We walked out of the library. At the bottom of the steps I said, "Thanks, Cary."

"Hey," he said. "It's only the beginning of a beautiful friendship."

I wasn't sure what he meant by that, but before I could ask, Cokie materialized.

"Cary," she said. "How nice to see you. I'm having a big party on Saturday night and I want everybody who is anybody at SMS to be there. And you too, of course, Mary Anne. Here, let me give you an invitation with an address on it."

I shifted my pack and felt the bump of the subscription cards against my arm. "Thanks," I said. "I'd love to come, Cokie."

Cokie, who'd been rummaging in her purse, looked up in surprise. I gave her a big smile and added, "You don't have to give me your address. I *know* where you live."

"I'll take it," said Cary, extracting the invitation from Cokie's fingers.

"Great," Cokie chirped. She smiled at Cary. Her smile disappeared as she turned to me. "And I'm glad you're going to come, Mary Anne. It'll be nice for you to get out."

I didn't answer. Cary and I watched Cokie walk away. "Going into enemy territory?" Cary murmured.

I patted the subscription cards. "Why not? I have her address," I answered.

He grinned. "And I have her cell phone."

"What?" Sure enough, Cary had Cokie's small, sleek, expensive cell phone in the palm of his hand. "When . . . how?"

"I have my methods, Watson. See you later."

He sauntered off, leaving me to stare, open-mouthed, after him.

I was glad he was on my side.

❋ Chapter 10

Maybe it was a day of plotting to get even with Cokie that made the nightmare so bad that night. I woke up with the smell of smoke in my nostrils and tears on my face. It took me a long time to convince myself that I didn't smell smoke, and that I wasn't in a burning house.

This made it hard to go back to sleep.

I wasn't the only one who was having trouble sleeping. I heard my father's footsteps go up and down the hall several times, and then I thought I heard the low murmur of the television set. My father does that sometimes when he can't sleep. He watches old movies on television.

Neither Dad nor I was in the best of moods at breakfast the next morning. Dad retreated behind the newspaper, coming out only to pour more coffee or say, "Listen to this" and read some particularly disagreeable news item.

I rolled my eyes every time he read something, but I didn't speak. Mostly I just drooped over my plate and felt tired from it all.

Sharon tried to lighten things up, but she didn't help. Her cheerfulness only made the gloom and doom hovering over the table seem worse.

Arriving at school to discover that Cokie had started another rumor about me didn't help either. This one was about how I had begged her for an invitation to her party when I'd found out that Logan was going to be there. Honestly, between making up lies about people and fixing elections, when did that girl have time to do her homework?

"This has to be stopped," Kristy said, meeting me in the hall. "I know you talked to Cary, but maybe I should speak to him."

"I can take care of it," I snapped. "I'm not a *total* wimp."

Kristy raised her eyebrows. "No. I guess you're not. Anyway, I'm going to tell people that this rumor is just another one of Cokie's desperate ploys to win the election."

"Good," I said. "Pass it along."

Claudia, Abby, and Stacey did their jobs well. By the time I ran into Logan after lunch, he said, "I heard Cokie's latest — and I also heard she'd doing it to get back at you for calling her on the election results."

"Yup," I said. "That's our Cokie."

Logan smiled that smile that still makes me feel a little breathless. "*Are* you going to Cokie's party?" he asked. "She's said to more than one person that you wouldn't dare show up."

Inside, the old Mary Anne was whimpering, "No, no, no. There's no way I'll go near Cokie's house!" But the new Mary Anne said, "I'll see you there."

"Cool," said Logan, and that was that.

Naturally, the Cokie-induced madness at SMS was the topic of much conversation at the BSC meeting that Wednesday afternoon. "If you're going to the party, I'm going to the party," Kristy announced as the meeting ended. "And Abby'll go too."

"I wish I could," said Claudia.

"Me too," said Stacey.

Automatically, I reached for the book where I

keep our baby-sitting jobs listed. But Stacey stopped me. "We know, we know, Mary Anne. We're sitting that night."

"I'll take notes," said Kristy. "Maybe even pictures. Mary Anne, why don't you come over to my house for dinner tonight and we can think of ways to make Cokie say she's sorry."

"I think being Cokie means never having to say you're sorry," I said.

I spent the rest of the evening at Kristy's in a much better mood. We'd already discussed party wear at the BSC meeting (and would again, I knew, at the meeting on Friday), so that left us free to think of outrageous schemes for making Cokie look dumb. Kristy worried that we might be walking into a trap, but I convinced her that Cokie was too focused on trying to win votes with the party.

"I mean, this is a big party," I said. "Plus, Cokie was shocked when I told her I'd show up."

"True. And Cokie's not subtle. If she was going to go after you in a big way, she'd already be dropping hints," Kristy agreed. "Speaking of going after Cokie, have you talked to Cary again?"

"No. And I haven't mailed the subscription cards either. Although if Cokie goes too far, she could be reading *Popular Mechanics* in triplicate very soon."

We laughed. We also agreed that we needed to do some party planning of the sneaky, Cary Retlin-mischief kind.

And then I realized what time it was.

I gasped. "Oh, no. I'm late. *Way* past curfew. I can't believe they haven't called yet."

"I'll get Charlie. He'll drive you," said Kristy, efficient as always. (Charlie is Kristy's oldest brother.) In no time, I'd been whisked into Charlie's car and ferried to my house.

My father opened the door as Charlie pulled up. I didn't like the way he stood there, unmoving, unspeaking, as I got out of the car and thanked Charlie and Kristy for the ride.

I didn't like the way he still didn't speak as I ran up the walk.

"I'm sorry," I panted. "Kristy and I totally lost track of time."

My father stepped to one side to let me in. He closed the door behind me with a little too much emphasis. "I'm aware of that."

"I'm sorry. It won't happen again." I was trying to edge away. "Uh, so where's Sharon?"

"Out."

"Past curfew too, huh?" I tried to make a joke.

Big mistake.

"Sharon's an adult. She called earlier to tell me she was running late. You are not an adult and apparently not responsible enough to be treated like one, since you didn't call."

Uh-oh.

"You knew where I was," I said feebly. "You could have called me."

"That's not the point. How could you worry me like that?" My father had reverted to his protective-father mode. And it was too much.

"If you were so worried," I said, "why didn't you just call Kristy's house? It's not like I was anywhere dangerous. I was *at Kristy's*."

"I don't appreciate that tone of voice from you."

"And I don't appreciate being set up in some kind of, some kind of, well, curfew trap. It wasn't like I was out drinking and smoking."

"That's it. I've had it."

"You've had it? *I've* had it. I said I was sorry. It's never happened before. It won't happen again. What do you want me to do?"

"I'll tell you what you're going to do. You're going to stay right here for the next two weeks. You're grounded."

I didn't answer. I turned and marched to my room. And I didn't close my door a little bit harder than necessary.

I slammed it.

❃ Chapter 11

I had been wrong when I'd told Kristy that Cokie's party was going to be a big one. It wasn't. It was extra-giant size. Majorly, extravagantly enormous.

This became apparent by the fact that Cokie spent all day Thursday handing out invitations. She invited the entire eighth grade.

"I'm doomed," I said at lunch. "Doomed. If I don't go to the party, it will look like I'm afraid of Cokie. And if I do, I'll have to sneak out of the house and lie to my father and Sharon."

"A curfew. Wow. Bummer," said Abby. Abby and her twin sister, Anna, don't really have a curfew or a lot of rules. Her father died a few years ago and she and her sister had to grow up fast. Now her mother works long hours so Abby and Anna have learned to be independent. I considered pointing out to my father that Abby didn't have a curfew and that she was the least likely person in the world to stay out late and do dumb things. But I knew what my father would say: "You're not Abby Stevenson."

And he was right. I wasn't. I was Mary Anne Spier. The overprotected.

I envied Abby's easygoing, make-the-rules-as-we-go family for a moment. I sighed.

"Can't you try talking to your father?" asked Claudia. "Explain the situation."

"He's still pretty angry at me," I answered. "I talked to Sharon and she said I should give him some time. Time! I don't have any time. The party is this Saturday. I have to be there. But I can't. . . . At least, I don't think I can."

"Sneaking out isn't hard," said Kristy. "I don't recommend it as the usual way to leave the house, but in an emergency, it might be unavoidable."

"You sneak out of your house at night?" Claudia asked Kristy.

"Not all the time," said Kristy, looking pained. "But I did once for that stupid initiation thing for the softball team. I was dumb to do it and I almost got into big trouble, but my point is, sneaking out isn't hard. Especially when your parents don't expect you to sneak out."

"I don't know," I said. I couldn't imagine myself creeping out of the house.

Stacey said, "Well, even if you don't go, Kristy and Abby will be there to represent us. And to do a few party activities of their own."

"Of the Cary Retlin kind." Kristy caught on immediately.

"Right," said Stacey.

"Where *is* Cary?" Claudia asked. "Have you talked to him about any of this?"

"No," I said. "Every time I see him, he seems to be going around a corner. I haven't been able to catch up with him."

"Typical Cary," remarked Kristy. "Well, we don't need him. We can make some party problems on our own, if we want to."

"Even if we don't want to, and I'm not sure I do," I said, "I don't mind thinking about it."

"Good." Kristy pulled out a piece of paper and a pen. "Let's get to work."

"We could have thirty-seven pizzas delivered to her house during the party," Claudia suggested.

Kristy wrote it down.

"Locking the bathroom doors from the inside is a good way to jam up a crowd," observed Stacey.

"Excellent," Kristy said, her pen flying.

"Lights out. Temporary but effective," said Abby.

"We'd have to find the fuse box," Kristy pointed out.

"It's probably in the basement," Abby said. "I'll bring a flashlight, just in case."

"Salt," said Claudia.

We looked at her. "In the food," she explained. "In the punch. Whatever."

"Possible," Kristy said.

I said, "There's always that lame one, you know, shaking up the soda cans."

"If Cokie's smart, she won't have cans of soda, just those big bottles," said Kristy.

"Who said Cokie was smart?" I muttered. I was on my way to deciding that it was all Cokie's fault I'd been grounded. After all, I wouldn't have been late if I hadn't had to spend so much time talking about her and her stupid party.

And I wouldn't even have had to consider going to her stupid party if she hadn't fixed the election and started all those rumors about me.

But if Cokie were so dumb, how come I was the one who was grounded?

I said more loudly, "In that movie *The Parent Trap* they have all kinds of great sabotage stuff."

Stacey said, "You're right. And in the old version, there's a scene where one of the girls cuts the back out of another girl's skirt, remember?"

"I don't think that's going to work on Cokie," Claudia said. "Even if you could manage it, her skirts are already pretty small."

"Fake vomit?" said Abby.

"That's something Alan Gray would do," Kristy answered.

"Hey!" Claudia exclaimed, wounded. She and Alan recently went to a dance together, much to Kristy's surprise. None of us is sure what will happen next with them.

"Well, still," said Abby. "A few of those little fake ants in the food, a spare rubber cockroach or two — I don't care how childish it is, it's still effective."

"This is true," I said. "Write it down, Kristy."

"Yes, ma'am!"

Cary was right about one thing, I thought. Planning ahead, even if you weren't going to follow through with something, gives you a real boost.

Anything could happen at the party. The worst could happen. It could be a disaster.

I smiled, visualizing it. Then I sighed, thinking that I would miss it.

I spent the rest of the day considering this. But it wasn't until I ran into Cary before last period that I realized just how hard and how seriously I had been entertaining the idea of sneaking out of the house.

"Still on for the party?" he asked.

"We have big plans for it," I said.

"So do I." He smiled. "I like the way Cokie is being lulled into thinking that everything is okay, don't you?"

I looked at Cary. Hard. But his face gave nothing away.

"Yes," I said. "I have a feeling it's going to be some party. I can hardly wait."

And that's when I knew that I, Mary Anne Spier, formerly the incredible shrinking girl, was going to sneak out of the house on Saturday night.

✱ Chapter 12

At 8:00 on Saturday night I yawned. "I'm tired," I said.

"So early?" Sharon asked.

I shrugged. I felt guilty about what I was planning to do. But I was also angry because I felt as if, somehow, it wasn't entirely my fault. Not logical, but there you have it.

My father said, "Stay up. There's a great old movie coming on at nine." He and Sharon had been engaged in an endless game of Scrabble in the den. Sharon kept beating my dad. I'd been pretending to read.

"No," I said. "Thanks anyway. I've had about all the Saturday night excitement I can stand."

My father frowned. Before the fire, I'd been sarcastic about once in my life. Now guilt was making me sarcastic. Cokie was making me sarcastic. My father was making me sarcastic.

The new Mary Anne was making me sarcastic. The old Mary Anne wanted to apologize. The new Mary Anne said, "Good night. See you tomorrow."

I gave my father a good-night peck on the cheek, gave the same to Sharon, and headed for my room.

I waited a few minutes. Then I got dressed. I opened the door to go to the bathroom to brush my teeth — and heard Sharon's footsteps in the hall.

Quickly I closed the door. If Sharon had seen me, she would have known something was up. I had no good explanation for changing out of sweatpants and one of her ratty old work shirts into my best new jeans and new favorite striped shirt.

I took off my jeans, grabbed my bathrobe, and wrapped it around me.

Sharon passed me on my way into the bathroom.

"Sleep well," she said.

"You too."

I brushed my teeth and put on my makeup. I opened the bathroom door — to find my father standing there.

"Dad!" I squeaked.

"Sorry. Didn't mean to startle you. I was about

to knock. Just wanted to make sure everything's okay."

Could he see the makeup? Smell the perfume? "I'm fine. Really," I said stiffly. " 'Night."

" 'Night, Mary Anne."

I practically dove back into my room. Then I collapsed onto my bed and thought.

I had two choices: I could go out the window — and climb down the maple tree outside it. Or I could sneak down the hall, down the stairs, through the living room, then into the kitchen and out the kitchen door without being heard or seen.

Be sneaky, I told myself. Think like a spy.

After several minutes of deliberation, I slid my window open and dropped my shoes and socks out of it, trying to make sure they landed away from the rosebushes directly below.

Then I rolled up the legs of my jeans, tightened the sash of my bathrobe, and picked up the water glass by my bed. If Sharon or my father caught me, I'd say I was going to the kitchen for some water.

I walked boldly downstairs and through the living room. I hovered outside the den door. I heard the murmur of voices and then I heard Sharon say, "Oops. I dropped one."

"I'll get it for you," my father said.

Sharon snorted. "And see what letter it is? I'll get it."

I heard the laughter in my father's voice as he said, "No. I insist."

Deciding that both Sharon and my father were looking down at the floor for a Scrabble piece instead of toward the door, I took a giant step across the den entrance.

I stopped and held my breath.

"Got it!" Sharon was triumphant.

"Yes, but it's my turn," my father answered.

I tiptoed into the kitchen, clutching the glass so tightly it's a wonder it didn't break.

I slipped the extra set of house keys off the key rack and cautiously unlocked the door.

Footsteps sounded in the hall.

Without thinking, I threw myself into the tiny space between the refrigerator and the wall, wedging myself in with the mop and broom. The broom slid forward. I grabbed it and yanked it back just as the kitchen light went on.

"Diet Coke or regular Coke?" my father's voice said.

"Regular," I heard Sharon call back.

I sucked in my breath and stood, panicked, holding the broom in one hand and the glass in the other. How would I ever explain what I was doing folded between the fridge and the wall?

Cabinet doors opened. Kitchen glasses clunked against the countertop. The refrigerator door swung back and I saw my father's foot beneath the bottom edge of it.

He took out ice trays and bottles and closed the door. I listened to the clink of ice against glass and the fizz of soda being poured over it. I heard him run water into the ice tray. Then he opened the door again, reloaded the ice tray, and put the bottles back inside.

It took forever and a day.

At last he walked out of the kitchen. I was about to leap out to safety when he muttered, "Uh-oh." Footsteps came back and then the light flicked off.

Then my father left the kitchen.

I waited a long, long time to make sure he wasn't coming back.

Finally, cautiously, I peered out. When I didn't see anybody, I bolted out (making sure the broom and mop didn't bolt with me), put my glass on the counter, opened the back door, and made my escape.

My heart was still pounding like the heart of a prisoner escaping from jail when I met Kristy and

Abby a few minutes later on the corner of Cokie's block.

"You made it," Kristy said.

"Of course," I replied with a calm I didn't feel. I'd had trouble finding one of my socks and finally had to go sockless. My bathrobe was hidden in the rosebushes. I hoped I could disentangle it when I got home.

Maybe I could wait until daylight. . . .

"Flashlight, salt, and plastic ants," said Abby, holding up her pack. "I do not come unprepared."

"Plastic vomit," Kristy said, looking sheepish. "Also, Vaseline. I have plans for the toilet seats, if we decide action is necessary."

"Great." I was forgetting about my Great Escape. "But not unless I say so."

"It's your party," said Kristy.

"Yeah. Only Cokie doesn't know it yet," Abby added.

"Then, let's go." I boldly led the way into the house of the enemy.

❋ Chapter 13

Cokie opened the door. "Mary Anne! How nice that you could get out."

I froze. Had Cokie found out I was grounded?

But I realized she was just being generally nasty as she smiled the same phony smile at Kristy and Abby. "And your faithful friends too!"

The way she said it, Abby and Kristy might have been dogs.

"We thought your little party would need all the help it could get," Abby said. She walked past Cokie into the house. "How do you do?"

I became aware of Cokie's parents hovering nearby. Somehow that reassured me. There were limits to what Cokie could do with her parents somewhere in the house. Weren't there?

Following Abby's lead, Kristy and I nodded and

smiled at Mr. and Mrs. Mason. They seemed perfectly nice. I wondered if they had considered the possibility that Cokie and their real baby had been switched in the hospital. Those things did happen, after all.

We walked for several miles down carpeted halls, past mirrors and vases of fresh flowers.

"Wow," I said. "This house is *almost* as big as yours, Kristy."

I said it loudly. I knew Cokie heard me and I knew it bothered her. But what could she say? It was her problem for thinking that the size of someone's house mattered.

By the time we entered the living room I realized that most of the rest of the SMS eighth grade was, in fact, at Cokie's house. It took me about two and a half seconds to spot Logan and Dorianne together by the CD player, sorting through the tunes.

My heart skipped and lurched. Seeing them together wasn't going to be as easy as I had hoped.

Kristy saw them too. She moved between them and me and said, "Let's go get something to drink."

"Yeah," Abby said. "I could do a Dew."

We passed Emily, Woody, and Woody's friend Trevor Sandbourne deep in conversation near one end of the refreshment table. Emily turned to us to grin and gesture. "Check it out," she said. "Martha Stewart meets wicked excess."

"Good grief," said Kristy.

A table spread with a white cloth lined one whole wall.

Abby said, "I've seen Bat Mitzvahs and sweet sixteens with spreads like this, but never an ordinary party."

"Everything but the waiters to pass around trays of hors d'oeuvres," Woody said.

I saw little quiches (at least I think that's what they were); and mushrooms, carrots, cauliflower, and celery sticks next to three kinds of dip. I saw a melon filled with fruit surrounded by even more dip. I saw at least a half-dozen platters fanned out with meat and cheese. Little bowls of pickles, mustard, and mayonnaise; trays of bread and rolls; and much, much more marched down the table. At the far end, rack upon rack of soda bottles and cups jostled a huge bowl of punch.

"Cokie really knows how to throw a party, doesn't she?" whispered Grace as she approached us.

Woody, polite and politic as always, said, "I could never throw a party like this."

"Well, don't just stand there," Grace said, giggling, "eat!"

"For once, I'm going to do what Grace says," Kristy muttered to me.

We picked up plates and moved down the table, then snagged seats at the far end of the room.

Logan and Dorianne had started dancing together. I saw Woody and Emily head for the dance floor. That seemed to be some kind of signal that it was okay to dance, because soon several other couples followed suit.

Cokie wasn't among them. I saw her flitting from group to group. She spoke to everybody and laughed a lot, throwing her head back as if SMS had suddenly become a school filled with amazingly witty people. Her teeth flashed. She swung her hair back and forth across her shoulders. She leaned close to the boys and touched their arms.

But no one asked her to dance. No one lingered long to talk to her except Grace and some of Cokie's other cronies.

Did Cokie notice that something was off? That people were wise to her phony friendliness? Did she realize that everyone was happy enough to eat her food and dance to her CDs, but that they weren't burning to be her friends?

I couldn't tell.

Kristy suddenly put her plate down. "I'm going to the bathroom," she said. "I'll be back."

"Don't do anything — " I started to say, meaning *No Acts of Sabotage*, but I didn't get the chance to finish. Kristy was already gone.

Then I saw Howie Johnson stop to watch her go and realized that Kristy had figured out, correctly, that Howie was headed toward her to ask her to dance. She had made her escape.

Howie turned back toward us.

"More punch?" Abby said, and leaped up and made her escape as well.

That left me. Howie didn't seem to mind. "Want to dance?"

"Uh, sure," I said, putting down my plate.

I stood up and stepped out into the crowd of couples. And then I realized that I was dancing with Howie Johnson.

Howie hopped around like a pogo stick and flapped his hands like elephant ears. I couldn't tell whether he was deliberately acting funny or whether that was actually the way he danced.

I glanced at Logan, who danced as gracefully and athletically as he played baseball or football or ran track. I hoped Dorianne appreciated that.

I made myself smile. But I was relieved when the dance was over and even more relieved when Howie said, "Thanks," and went off in search of another victim.

I didn't get to sit down, though. At least not right away. Out of nowhere, Cary Retlin slid up to me and said, "Dance."

I couldn't tell if it was a question or a command, but I nodded. He was a significantly better dancer than Howie. I actually found myself beginning to have a good time.

When the music stopped, Cary walked with me back to where I'd been sitting. Kristy and Abby had returned.

I gave them a look that said *traitors*, for having left me alone with Howie before.

Cary bowed with a flourish. "Ladies," he said. "Is the game afoot?"

"Not without the go-ahead from Mary Anne," said Kristy.

"Ah," said Cary. "Well, then . . . I think I'm in need of a little sustenance."

"If you mean food," said Abby, "go for it."

"I shall return." Cary did his disappearing act.

It was at that moment that Cokie made her

move. I'd relaxed. I'd forgotten to watch where she was. So had Kristy and Abby.

I realized later that Cokie had to have planned it. The music stopped completely, and it was Grace who was by the CD player.

Cokie laughed loudly into the silence. Very loudly. It was the sort of laugh that makes people look at you, wondering what's so funny.

She wasted no time letting people know that I was the joke.

"Poor Mary Anne," she said to her cronies. "Trying so *hard* to get Logan's attention, throwing herself at anybody who'll dance with her. It's pathetic. I feel sorry for her, don't you?"

More heads turned as Cokie's words pierced the quiet.

Kristy dropped her plate and stood. Abby, who was already up, rocked slightly on the balls of her feet. I'd seen that stance in the past — right before Abby leveled a goalie with the blast of a soccer ball.

"Wait," I said, trying to gather my wits.

Kristy balled her hands into fists, but she didn't move, and I registered the amazing fact that I, Mary Anne Spier, was bossing around the bossiest person on earth.

Abby continued to rock gently, but she didn't move.

I thought of all the snappy comebacks I'd wished for over the past few days — no, over all the years I'd known Cokie. I thought of saying, "You define pathetic, Cokie. In fact, your picture is next to the definition in the dictionary."

I opened my mouth. "Cokie," I said in a loud voice. "I heard what you said."

Cokie turned. "So?" she said. "I was just telling the truth."

"No," I said. "*I'll* tell *you* the truth. You are mean. Why? Why do you work so hard at being nasty and saying horrible things about people? There's no reason for it. Making fun of people and spreading rumors about them doesn't make you look cool. Do you think it does?"

"I never — " Cokie began furiously.

I kept right on going. I steamrollered her. "It doesn't make people like you. It makes you look stupid and petty and mean. And you know what? If you keep acting like this, you will *never* be Most Likely to Succeed. You won't be likely to succeed at all . . . because people will see the real Cokie. They'll know you for what you really are."

The room was truly silent now.

Then, as Cokie sputtered and turned red, Kristy and Abby started to clap.

The sound startled me. I'd forgotten where I was. I looked away from Cokie as Logan joined in. Then Dorianne. Then Emily let out a whoop. I saw Cary raise his hands to applaud over his head.

And then the whole room was applauding. I heard "All right!" and "You go, Mary Anne" and "That's telling her."

Cokie lost it completely. "Stop it! Stop it. This is *my* party and you can't do this!"

Cary stepped up to Grace, took the CD out of her hand, and slipped it into the player.

"STOP IT!" Cokie screamed, but now the music drowned her out.

Someone started laughing, and then Kristy and Abby dragged me out into the middle of the floor and we began to dance.

Cary danced up next to me. "Not bad, Mary Anne," he said. "I'd say that by telling the truth, you just got the sweetest revenge of all."

And he was right.

❋ Chapter 14

"Supercalifragilisticexpealidocious . . ." sang Kristy.

Abby and I sang along with her. The party hadn't lasted long after I'd confronted Cokie. The last we'd seen of her, she'd been stomping out of the room.

I'd been giddy with my newfound power — the power to stand up for myself — all the way home. From the sound of it, Kristy and Abby were a little giddy too.

We parted at the corner.

To my surprise, Kristy leaned over and gave me a quick hug. "You did good," she said.

"Don't get all sentimental," Abby warned her. "You'll make Mary Anne cry."

I smiled. I'd almost felt a tear come to my eye. But happiness washed over me again. I could face anything. Bring on the lions and tigers and bears!

Still in a state of bliss, I walked up to the back door of my house, slipped the key into the lock, slid the door open, and stepped inside. I closed it as quietly as I could and put the key back in its place.

The kitchen lights came on.

I jumped four thousand feet into the air, made a noise as if a giant mouse had run across my foot, and fell back against the door, my hand clapped over my mouth.

My father was standing in the kitchen. He did *not* look happy.

"Well," he said. "Welcome home."

I dropped my hand.

"Thank you," I said, because I couldn't think of anything else to say.

"Where have you been?" he asked.

"To a party at Cokie Mason's house."

My father was shaking his head. "I don't believe it." Shake, shake. "I just don't believe it." Shake. "I can't believe you would so blatantly disobey me."

"I'm sorry," I said. And I was. But I didn't stop there. "I had to go, though. Especially when you grounded me unfairly in the first place."

"Oh, so it's my fault, is it?" My father's face became a thundercloud.

"Mine — and yours," I said. "It takes two to make a mistake."

"I didn't make a mistake! I'm your father and I know what's best for you."

"Grounding me wasn't best for me," I shot back. "How can doing something so unfair be best for me?"

Our voices were loud.

Okay. We were shouting.

That's when Sharon flew into the kitchen. "That's enough," she said. "Be quiet, both of you. Now!"

That got my father's attention. He blinked. "Sharon?" he said.

"Sit!" she ordered. She pointed at a chair. "And Mary Anne, you sit there."

My father, watching Sharon as if she were a fire-cracker about to go off, sat. Feeling much the same, I sat down too.

"Listen to me. This is not a fight about curfew and this is not a fight about being grounded," Sharon said.

"But — "

"Richard, let me finish."

My father clamped his lips together. Wow, I thought. Sharon was *brave*.

"It is *so* obvious," she said. "And I'm tired of standing aside and letting two very scared people who love each other very much tear each other to pieces. Richard — did you know Mary Anne is still having nightmares about the fire?"

"No." My father looked even more shocked.

"She is. I hear her waking in the night, but she won't admit it. Because, I suspect, she is trying to keep you from worrying about her."

I looked down at my hands, which I had clasped on the table in front of me.

"And, Mary Anne, your father has become the house ghost. He wanders around all night because he can't sleep."

"I heard you a few times," I said. "But I didn't know it was so bad."

"Almost every night," my father admitted.

"He gets up, he checks on you, he checks to make sure the fire alarm is working, that the oven is turned off, that things are unplugged. He lies awake and worries that next time he won't be able to save us. Don't you, Richard?"

My father nodded.

"So what do you do, Richard? You start trying to protect Mary Anne from everything. You're treating her like she's a little girl again. But she's not. She's a very mature thirteen-year-old. Don't forget, she had the presence of mind to save Tigger."

I'd never thought about it that way.

"So you've both got to put this behind you. Richard, Mary Anne, you can't protect each other from everything in the world. Life goes on, and you have to go with it. And, incidentally, it's not just you two against the world anymore. Don't forget that I'm part of this family too."

Sharon stopped speaking.

We stared at her. Then my eyes met my father's. I realized it was true. He was scared, as scared as I was.

"Mary Anne . . ." my father began.

"I'll leave you two alone," said Sharon.

"Wait," I told her. "Stay."

My father reached up and caught the sash of her robe. He pointed at the chair on the other side of him. "Sit," he said, and we all had a shaky laugh.

So we talked, for what seemed like half the night. We drank hot chocolate, and Dad and I apologized to Sharon for how tense we'd been making things lately. We agreed that we had to be more open about everything. And we decided we'd make a new beginning together, right here, right now.

"You're still grounded," my father said as I stood up.

"Richard," said Sharon.

"Until Monday morning," he added. "So don't sneak off anywhere tomorrow, okay?"

"Okay," I agreed.

And I went upstairs to bed and had the dream again. Only this time, I didn't shrink. I opened the door, walked through the smoke, and out of the house. We were all safe.

It wasn't a pleasant dream. But it wasn't a nightmare anymore.

✿ Chapter 15

I spent all day Sunday thinking things over. By Monday morning, I'd figured out that while I wasn't the old, shrinking Mary Anne, I wasn't the new, tough, vengeful Mary Anne either, the one who carried around the subscriptions and dreamed of stuffing Cokie into her locker.

But I had changed. I knew that Cokie, no matter what she said, could never make me cry again. I knew that when I got in a tough spot, I'd stand up and try to fight my way out. I wouldn't weep and wring my hands and wait for someone to save me. Sometimes it was fine to get angry and to fight back.

I'd never be like Cokie, or even Kristy or Abby. I'd never start a fight or leap into battle like a demon soccer warrior.

But I would stand my ground.

So when Cokie shot me an evil look in the hall on Monday morning, I didn't worry about it. I didn't respond at all. I just walked on by.

We voted for the Most and Best that morning. Mr. Fiske decided to count the ballots himself, with some help from the assistant principal. I guess that's what they spent their lunch hour doing.

I spent mine talking to people I didn't normally see at lunch. Logan stopped by the table to say hello, and that was okay. Emily came by, and so did Woody and half a dozen other people, just to say hello.

I didn't see Cary. I suspected he was somewhere, setting up mischief, making the world a more complicated and interesting place.

Mr. Fiske announced the winners of the election that day before school let out.

I'm not going to tell you every winner, but here are the most important ones:

Claudia won Best Artist.

Abby and Logan got Best Athletes.

Cary and Alan tied for Wittiest.

Emily was voted Most Likely to Succeed *and* Most Intelligent.

Kristy got Most Likely to Be Elected President.

Amazingly, Stacey didn't win Class Style Setter. She was chosen Most Likely to be Seen in Beverly Hills.

I didn't win anything, but then I hadn't expected to.

Cokie didn't win anything either. Not a single thing. And I think she still expected to. I saw her face as we walked out of the building.

It was not a pretty sight. I don't think whatever she was ranting about in poor Grace's ear was very pretty either.

Cokie didn't see me then, and I was glad. I almost felt sorry for her.

Almost.

After school, Kristy, Claudia, Stacey, Abby, and I headed downtown to the Rosebud Cafe for celebratory junk food. We settled into one of the old-fashioned booths and Kristy said, "Mary Anne, this is on us."

I blushed. I grinned. I said, "In that case, I want a double chocolate fudge sundae with extra nuts and whipped cream."

We were just digging in when Dorianne and Logan walked through the door.

Logan saw us and stopped, looked a little uncertain.

I was able to smile and wave and act perfectly normal. For a moment, I was so carried away with how easy it was that I almost invited them to sit with us.

But then I realized that I wasn't ready for that. Not yet.

They sat down across the room and I discovered Kristy watching me. I made a little face and smiled.

Kristy looked relieved. She raised her chocolate mint chip shake and said, "I'd like to propose a toast . . . to Mary Anne, who's the real Most Likely to Succeed."

"Hear, hear!" said Abby, and we all drank to that.

L. GODWIN

Ann M. Martin

About the Author

ANN MATTHEWS MARTIN was born on August 12, 1955. She grew up in Princeton, NJ, with her parents and her younger sister, Jane.

Although Ann used to be a teacher and then an editor of children's books, she's now a full-time writer. She gets ideas for her books from many different places. Some are based on personal experiences. Others are based on childhood memories and feelings. Many are written about contemporary problems or events.

All of Ann's characters, even the members of the Baby-sitters Club, are made up. (So is Stoneybrook.) But many of her characters are based on real people. Sometimes Ann names her characters after people she knows; other times she chooses names she likes.

In addition to the Baby-sitters Club books, Ann Martin has written many other books for children. Her favorite is *Ten Kids, No Pets* because she loves big families and she loves animals. Her favorite BSC book is *Kristy's Big Day*. (Kristy is her favorite baby-sitter.)

Ann M. Martin now lives in New York with her cats, Gussie, Woody, and Willy, and her dog, Sadie. Her hobbies are reading, sewing, and needlework — especially making clothes for children.

Friends Forever

Look for #9

KRISTY AND THE KIDNAPPER

Two of the guards ran down the stairs toward the basement and the indoor parking garage. The other two ran up.

I had a gut feeling that I should follow the ones who had headed downstairs, so I did. As soon as we burst through the door into the parking garage, I spotted David. The man in the dark clothes was dragging him toward a long black car. "There he is!" I yelled, pointing. The guards took off toward the man, who pushed David to the ground and took off, running.

"David!" I cried. "Are you okay?" I sprinted to help him up as the security guards chased after the kidnapper. The young woman from the reception desk appeared next to me; she must have followed us.

"I'll help you," she said, taking David's other arm. We supported him as he rose shakily to his feet.

"Are you okay?" I repeated.

David thought for a minute. "I guess so," he said, sounding dazed. "Just a little bruised." He took a few limping steps. "I don't think anything's broken."

We helped him hobble back to the stairway. As we made our way back to the lobby, the security guards reappeared — empty-handed.

"Did you catch him?" I asked, even though it was obvious that they hadn't.

They shook their heads.

The kidnapper was still out there somewhere.

Check out what's new with your old friends.

THE BABY-SITTERS CLUB®

Collect 'em all!

100 (and more) Reasons to Stay Friends Forever!

More titles... ▶

The Baby-sitters Club titles continued...

☐ MG22881-1	#97	Claudia and the World's Cutest Baby	$3.99
☐ MG22882-X	#98	Dawn and Too Many Sitters	$3.99
☐ MG69205-4	#99	Stacey's Broken Heart	$3.99
☐ MG69206-2	#100	Kristy's Worst Idea	$3.99
☐ MG69207-0	#101	Claudia Kishi, Middle School Dropout	$3.99
☐ MG69208-9	#102	Mary Anne and the Little Princess	$3.99
☐ MG69209-7	#103	Happy Holidays, Jessi	$3.99
☐ MG69210-0	#104	Abby's Twin	$3.99
☐ MG69211-9	#105	Stacey the Math Whiz	$3.99
☐ MG69212-7	#106	Claudia, Queen of the Seventh Grade	$3.99
☐ MG69213-5	#107	Mind Your Own Business, Kristy!	$3.99
☐ MG69214-3	#108	Don't Give Up, Mallory	$3.99
☐ MG69215-1	#109	Mary Anne To the Rescue	$3.99
☐ MG05988-2	#110	Abby the Bad Sport	$3.99
☐ MG05989-0	#111	Stacey's Secret Friend	$3.99
☐ MG05990-4	#112	Kristy and the Sister War	$3.99
☐ MG05911-2	#113	Claudia Makes Up Her Mind	$3.99
☐ MG05911-2	#114	The Secret Life of Mary Anne Spier	$3.99
☐ MG05993-9	#115	Jessi's Big Break	$3.99
☐ MG05994-7	#116	Abby and the Worst Kid Ever	$3.99
☐ MG05995-5	#117	Claudia and the Terrible Truth	$3.99
☐ MG05996-3	#118	Kristy Thomas, Dog Trainer	$3.99
☐ MG05997-1	#119	Stacey's Ex-Boyfriend	$3.99
☐ MG05998-X	#120	Mary Anne and the Playground Fight	$3.99
☐ MG50063-5	#121	Abby in Wonderland	$3.99
☐ MG50064-3	#122	Kristy in Charge	$3.99
☐ MG50174-7	#123	Claudia's Big Party	$3.99
☐ MG50175-5	#124	Stacey McGill...Matchmaker?	$3.99
☐ MG50179-8	#125	Mary Anne in the Middle	$3.99
☐ MG50349-9	#126	The All-New Mallory Pike	$4.50
☐ MG50350-2	#127	Abby's Un-Valentine	$4.50
☐ MG50351-0	#128	Claudia and the Little Liar	$4.50
☐ MG45575-3		Logan's Story Special Edition Readers' Request	$3.25
☐ MG47118-X		Logan Bruno, Boy Baby-sitter Special Edition Readers' Request	$3.50
☐ MG47756-0		Shannon's Story Special Edition	$3.50
☐ MG47686-6		The Baby-sitters Club Guide to Baby-sitting	$3.25
☐ MG47314-X		The Baby-sitters Club Trivia and Puzzle Fun Book	$2.50
☐ MG48400-1		BSC Portrait Collection: Claudia's Book	$3.50
☐ MG22864-1		BSC Portrait Collection: Dawn's Book	$3.50
☐ MG69181-3		BSC Portrait Collection: Kristy's Book	$3.99
☐ MG22865-X		BSC Portrait Collection: Mary Anne's Book	$3.99
☐ MG48399-4		BSC Portrait Collection: Stacey's Book	$3.50
☐ MG92713-2		The Complete Guide to The Baby-sitters Club	$4.95
☐ MG47151-1		The Baby-sitters Club Chain Letter	$14.95
☐ MG48295-5		The Baby-sitters Club Secret Santa	$14.95
☐ MG45074-3		The Baby-sitters Club Notebook	$2.50
☐ MG44783-1		The Baby-sitters Club Postcard Book	$4.95

Available wherever you buy books...or use this order form.

Scholastic Inc., P.O. Box 7502, 2931 E. McCarty Street, Jefferson City, MO 65102

Please send me the books I have checked above. I am enclosing $_____ (please add $2.00 to cover shipping and handling). Send check or money order– no cash or C.O.D.s please.

Name _____ Birthdate_____

Address _____

City_____ State/Zip _____

BSC998